Published by Ladybird Books Ltd
27 Wrights Lane London W8 5TZ
A Penguin Company
3 5 7 9 10 8 6 4 2
© Ladybird Books Ltd MCMXCIX

LADYBIRD and the device of a Ladybird are
trademarks of Ladybird Books Ltd

© Disney MCMXCIX

Based on the Pooh stories by A A Milne
(copyright The Pooh Properties Trust)

Printed in Italy

Winnie the Pooh lived in a little house deep in the Hundred Acre Wood.

Pooh was *very* fond of honey. He could lick out a honey pot until there was nothing left except a little bit of stickiness round the rim. Pooh was so greedy that he could eat a whole pot of honey and *still* feel hungry!

One morning, just as Pooh was deciding how to spend his day, he heard his clock chime.

"Now," said Pooh, "that means it's time for me to do something. If only I could remember what that something was!"

Pooh began to think very hard. "Think, think, think," he said to himself, tapping his head. Then, he suddenly remembered. "Of course! It's time for my stoutness exercises."

Pooh stood in front of his mirror. He hummed a tune so that the exercises wouldn't seem such hard work.

"I go up, down, touch the ground,
Which puts me in the mood,
Up, down, touch the ground,
In the mood for lots of food!"

Pooh stretched his short arms up in the air, then bent down to touch his toes. Even though Pooh tried very hard, he couldn't quite reach them!

Suddenly, Pooh heard a loud
r-i-p-p-i-n-g sound. He turned round
and saw that one of his seams had
burst open.

"Oh, fluff and stuff!" said Pooh,
crossly. He pulled the thread and
tied it in a tight knot. "There, that's
better," he said. "Now, where was I?"
Pooh thought for a moment. "Oh,
yes! Time for honey!"

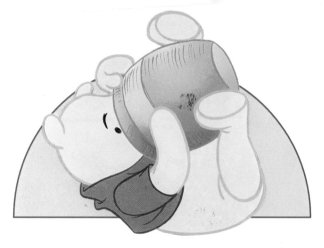

Pooh looked in his cupboard. There was only one honey pot left with hardly any honey in it.

"Bother!" said Pooh. "Only the sticky parts left." He put his head inside the pot to lick out the last little bits.

Suddenly, Pooh stood up. He had heard a buzzing noise. "The only reason that I know of for making a buzzing noise," he said to himself, "is because you're a bee!

"And the only reason for being a bee," Pooh went on, "is to make honey. And the only reason for making honey is so *I* can eat it!"

Pooh opened his front door and followed the bee outside. He watched it fly up into the sky and then disappear into a hole in a tree. *That must be a honey tree!* thought Pooh, and decided to climb it.

As Pooh climbed the honey tree, he hummed a little tune to himself.

"Hum dum dee dum,
Because my tumbly's very rumbly,
It's time for something sweet to eat,
Hum dee dum dum dum!"

Pooh climbed higher… and higher… and higher. He was so busy climbing and humming that he didn't notice how thin the branches were.

All of a sudden, there was a loud –
CRACK! The branch Pooh was sitting
on snapped. Down, down, down he
fell, bouncing and tumbling until –
BUMP!

He landed in a prickly gorse bush.
Poor old Pooh! He crawled out of
the bush and picked the prickles
from his fur.

Pooh was now a very cross, very hungry little bear. He sat down to think of another way to get the honey from the honey tree.

He thought and he thought. And the first person he thought of was Christopher Robin.

Christopher Robin lived in another
part of the Hundred Acre Wood.
Pooh knew that Christopher Robin
always tried to help his friends with
their problems, so he decided to go
and see him.

Pooh found Christopher Robin helping Eeyore. Poor Eeyore's tail had come off again.

Very gently, Christopher Robin tapped Eeyore's tail back in place with his hammer. Owl, Kanga and Roo watched.

Eeyore waved his tail to and fro. "It's working!" cried Roo, happily.

"Well, so it is," said Eeyore. "I know it's not much of a tail, but I am rather attached to it."

"Good morning," said Pooh.

"Good morning, Pooh," his friends replied.

"What are you looking for, Pooh Bear?" asked Christopher Robin.

"I wonder," said Pooh, "Can I borrow your blue balloon?"

"What do you want a blue balloon for?" asked Christopher Robin.

Pooh put his paw to his mouth and said in a whisper, "Honey!"

"But you don't get honey from a balloon," said Christopher Robin.

Pooh smiled. "I do," he said.

Then, Pooh found a muddy puddle.
He rolled and rolled in it until he
was black all over!

"Isn't this a clever disguise!" he said
to Christopher Robin.

"But what are you supposed to be,
Pooh?" Christopher Robin asked.

"A little, black rain cloud, of course!"
said Pooh. "The blue balloon will
look like part of the sky and the bees
will think that I'm just a rain cloud
drifting by."

"Silly old bear," said Christopher
Robin. But he gave Pooh his balloon
anyway.

Pooh took the balloon and almost at once a gust of wind lifted him up into the air.

As he drifted up towards the top of the tree, he started to sing a song.

"I'm a little black rain cloud,
Floating under the honey tree.
I'm a little black rain cloud,
Don't pay any attention to me!"

Soon, Pooh was very close to where
the honey was. Some of the bees
started buzzing angrily around him.

"Christopher Robin!" called Pooh. "I think the bees suspect something!"

"Perhaps they think you're after their honey," said Christopher Robin.

"Maybe," said Pooh. "You never can tell with bees." And he tried singing his rain cloud song again.

But the more Pooh sang, the louder the bees buzzed. Pooh stretched out his paw and reached into the hole in the tree. He scooped out some delicious honey. The bees began to buzz very angrily indeed!

"Christopher Robin!" Pooh called.
"You could help me to trick the
bees! Put up your umbrella and say,
'Oh, my, it looks like rain!'"

Christopher Robin opened his big
umbrella. He walked up and down
saying, "Oh, my, it looks like rain!
Oh, my, it looks like rain!"

But the bees buzzed just as loudly as
before. All of a sudden, they
swarmed out of the tree, straight
towards Pooh and his balloon.

Pooh didn't like the look of all those angry bees flying towards him. "Christopher Robin!" he called, "I've decided these are the *wrong* sort of bees!"

As Pooh tried to scramble away, the knot on the end of his balloon came undone. The air rushed out of the balloon and Pooh found himself tumbling towards the ground.

"Christopher Robin! I think I'm coming down now!" he shouted.

Pooh came whizzing down through
the branches and landed safely in
Christopher Robin's arms.

But the bees were still very angry
with Pooh.

Luckily, Christopher Robin had an idea. He held Pooh very tightly and began to run away. The angry bees chased after them.

Christopher Robin ran and ran until he reached the muddy puddle. He and Pooh jumped in and hid under Christopher Robin's umbrella.

The bees buzzed angrily around,
looking for Christopher Robin and
Pooh. But they couldn't see them.
The umbrella made a *very* good
hiding place!

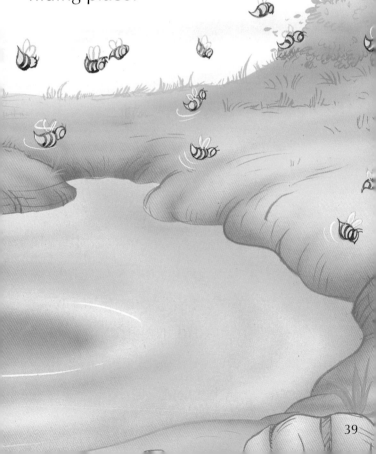

At last, the bees flew back to their tree. Christopher Robin and Pooh crept out from underneath the umbrella. Now, they looked just like *two* little black rain clouds!

"Oh, thank you, Christopher Robin," said Pooh. He was very glad that the bees had gone away.

"Silly old bear," laughed Christopher Robin and gave Pooh a big hug.

"I know," said Christopher Robin. "Let's have some tea and honey."

"What a good idea!" said Pooh.

Christopher Robin gave Pooh a full pot of honey and Pooh ate and ate until his tummy was full.

Pooh was a very happy, very sticky little bear. He had had a terrible adventure with the bees, but the day had ended wonderfully after all!